P9-CMS-133

WALLY
the WORDWORM

CLIFTON FADIMAN

WALLY the *WORDWORM*

illustrated by
LISA ATHERTON

Stemmer House
PUBLISHERS, INC.

Owings Mills, Maryland

Inquiries should be directed to
Stemmer House Publishers, Inc.
2627 Caves Road
Owings Mills, Maryland, 21117

A Barbara Holdridge book
Printed and bound in the United States of America
First Edition

Library of Congress Cataloging in Publication Data
Fadiman, Clifton, 1904-
    Wally the Wordworm.

    "A Barbara Holdridge book"—T.p. verso.
    Summary: A worm with a voracious appetite for words
who has grown bored with those he finds in the
tabloids, discovers the dictionary where his flagging
appetite revives. Includes puns, puzzles, and plays
on words.
    [1. Vocabulary—Fiction] I. Atherton, Lisa, ill.
II. Title.
PZ7.F13Wal   1983   [Fic]   83-9181
ISBN 0-88045-038-X

FOREWORD

WHEN I WAS ELEVEN YEARS OLD the only sports I was any good at—not *very* good, just ok—were chinning the bar and high jumping. I don't remember what my best jump was. What I do remember is that, after I had failed to clear the bar, the gym teacher would often say, kindly, "Well, let's lower it a couple of inches and start over." And I'd always get sore and refuse the easier jump. I figured that unless I kept on trying to do something a little too *hard* for me, I'd never get any better.

Well, I didn't get much better but I still think my idea a good one.

That idea lies back of this little book about Wally the Wordworm. I wrote it because I hated—just simply *hated*—books for children in which the words were supposed to suit their age, so that they'd never come across a word too "hard" for them. You don't learn that way, any more than you learn to high-jump by keeping the bar so low you can always clear it.

But it isn't just *learning* that matters. Words are *fun*, also—even words that you may never use again. Or words that look or sound odd. Or words that are interesting just because they're long or hard. If you add an l to **word**, you get **world.** And that's what a new word is—a tiny new world, opening up new meanings, new feelings, new perspectives (try looking up "perspectives." Oh—you *know* what it means? Sorry).

Wally, as you'll see, is an explorer, a word explorer. And a world explorer. I invented him some years ago and found that children liked him. Then the book went out of print. But I continued to get dozens (maybe hundreds) of letters from children and parents asking how they could get the book. And so here's a new edition with new pictures.

And, I hope, a lot of words that will be new to you and fun to fool around with.

Santa Barbara, California   Clifton Fadiman
May 1983

Wally the Wordworm was still hungry.
He'd already eaten: The headlines on
Page One of the morning newspaper.
(Quickly swallowed.)

Six Good Humor wrappers — just the
wrappers (PEANUT BRITTLE and
CARAMEL CRUNCH were the only
satisfying ones — they were words you
could really chew!) *And —*

A picture book with only seventy different words in it — all   short,
flat,
bare,
dull,
poor,
thin,
old ones that kept repeating themselves. They were good enough for a stupid worm, for a slow worm, for a worm who didn't care about real nourishment. But not good enough for Wally.

       "I'm still hungry," said he.

       "In fact, I am VORACIOUS!"

You see, Wally liked New Words,

BIG words,

Short, funny words,

Words that

S T R E T C H E D with

sound and meaning,
Words that make
interesting noises
inside your head.

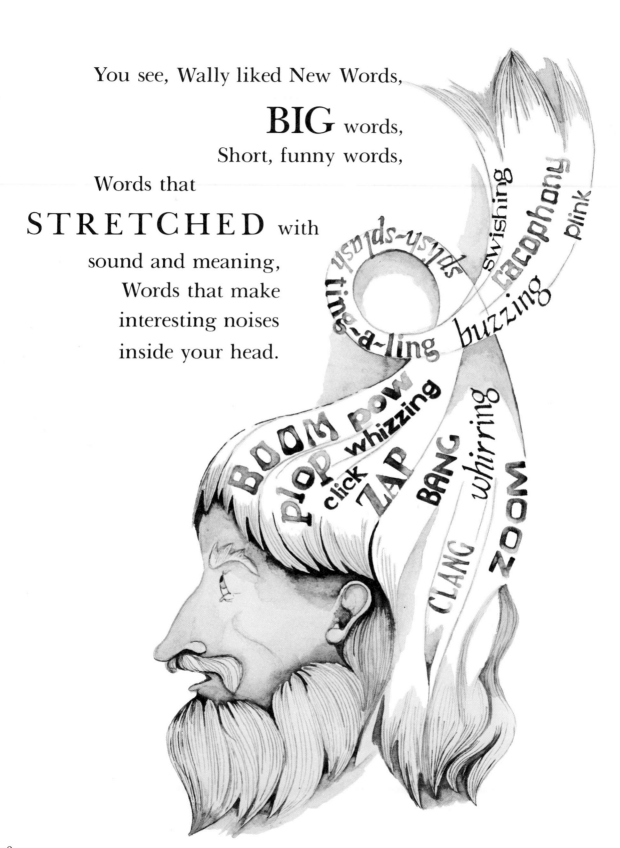

Words with strange faces that just *look*
interesting, like

and

and

Houyhnhnm

which you can't very well
pronounce unless you whinny
like a horse, and which *is* the
name of a fine race of talking
horses that can be found in a book
called *Gulliver's Travels.*

Wally the Wordworm not only liked
to eat words, he liked to

 **meet** them

 **greet** them

And **repeat repeat repeat** them.

So he slithered and slathered
And wiggled and waggled his
way into the library until he
found a big fat book called

DICTIONARY

This book was filled, stuffed,
packed, bulging, crammed,
and jammed with words of
all shapes and sizes.

"Hmm" said Wally, and
"Ha" said Wally, and
"Ho ho" said Wally, and
"Whoops" said Wally.

"Just my dish . . . just my dish."
And he licked his lips and crawled inside. He started near the back with a word just right for a hungry, growing worm:

SESQUIPEDALIAN

said Wally. "That means *long word* and looks like it, too." This went down pretty well and Wally looked around for another sesquipedalian.

He'd heard of
Antidisestablishmentarianism
(you probably have, too),
and he was surprised
not to find it.

"Hmmm,"
said Wally with a worried look.
And he had to settle for

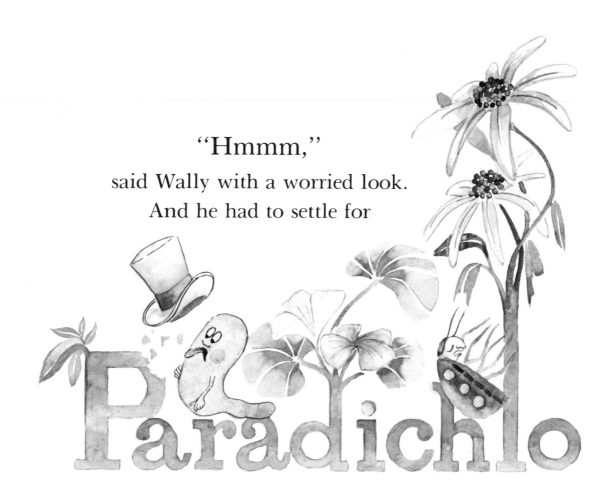

Paradichlo

robenzene

which tasted pretty bad.
(Look it up and you'll see why.)

Now Wally started to glide around
in the Dictionary, looking for a little
exercise. He found it with

He did a few
worm turns, and
ended up head
over heels at

SOMER SAULT

"Whew, pretty warm," said Wally, wiping his brow, and he ate only the last syllable. (Guess why.)

SOMERSAU

Next he wanted something that would go down easy. He passed by SOUP, and slithered into SLOOP which is a sailboat. It sailed down fine. Wally was beginning to feel rather full. (A worm tries to avoid bellyaches, just as an elephant hates a cold in the nose, and the giraffe, a stiff neck.) "All I need now is a little dessert," said Wally. "Something very light."

He turned the pages and found
"Now, that's the kind of word I like for
dessert," said Wally. "It's new, and fresh,
And it makes me laugh when I say
it — *dwindle*. I'll give it a try."
First he ate the big D in Dwindle.

"Capital eating," said Wally,
    who was fond of jokes like that.

            That left

    Then he ate the W.

            That left

    Then he ate the I.

            That left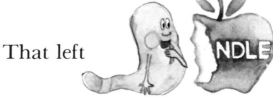

    Then he ate the N.

That left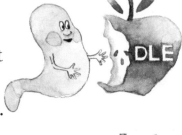

Then he ate the D.

That left

Then he ate the L.

That left

Then he ate the E.

"Good to the last spot,"
said Wally, and he ate that, too.

"And this,"
remarked Wally,
taking a bow,
"is how
DWINDLE dwindled.
A most enjoyable word lessen!"

20

Though Wally was in the D's and *decidedly done* with his *dining*, he thought he'd do a little more exploring. It wasn't much of a slither to make his way back to the beginning of the Dictionary. Here he found a word that opens all kinds of doors:

"ABRACADABRA," said Wally, waving his scarf at all those A's. They kept coming up again and again. ABRACADABRA, it looked like a fine word to practice his gymnastics on. He wondered whether he could touch all the A's *without* touching any other letter.

ABRACADABRA

He did it!

"Flexible character," said Wally.

Now Wally was feeling proud and a bit frisky.

He flipped through the pages. "Even a worm will turn," he said and stopped at the P's. Here he met a word that was absolutely new to him:

The Dictionary told him that a palindrome is a word or verse or sentence that reads the same backward or forward, like MADAM.

Well, of course, Wally had to test this for himself, so first he crawled forward from M to M and then crawled backward from M to M, and was pleased to discover that the Dictionary was right — either way, he spelled out MADAM.

After a while he wasn't sure whether he was coming or going. It was easy to think of words like PUP or TOT or GAG, and look them up, and palindrome on them.

But these exercises were too simple for a smart
worm. By great good luck on his next palindrome
hunt he discovered DEIFIED. "Neat," cried
Wally. He could hardly believe it. He crawled
forward, letter by letter, and he crawled backward,
letter by letter, repeating the performance a dozen
times, and each time good old DEIFIED
spelled itself correctly — it was magic.

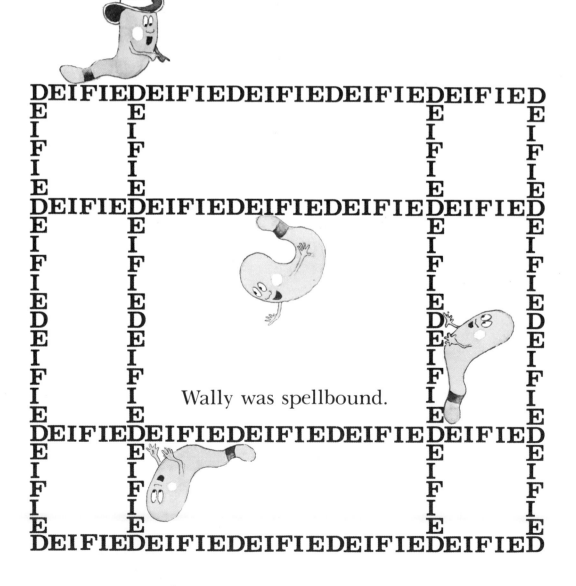

Wally was spellbound.

Wally's next experience was a startling one. He had
just finished an easy run on MOM which the
Dictionary listed as [Colloq.], mother, and
somehow or other he found himself upside down
on the page, looking *down* on MOM. At first
he couldn't believe his eyes. Then he let out
a whoop. What do you think he whooped?
WOW! But, though he did a lot of exploring,
he couldn't find another word that looked
as sensible standing on its head as it did on
its feet. Can you find one?

How about NOON?

25

Wally wriggled himself around till he was
right side up again, and decided to go on
a big word hunt for animals. "A SAFARI
in the Dictionary," he said with a gleam
in his eye. Wally was tired of cats, and
dogs, and cows, and horses. He wanted
big game, the stranger the better!

He went back to the A's and met the

ALLIGATOR who made it quite clear
that he had a shorter and blunter snout
than the crocodile. Wally flipped forward
to CROCODILE for he'd always confused
the two creatures. He discovered that the
crocodile, with the longer snout, got its
name from two Greek words, meaning
"pebble worm." This gave Wally a
pleasant family feeling. "Makes me feel
worm all over," he said.

ANACONDA  CONDOR

He went back to ANACONDA and wondered whether if you married it off to a certain large vulture found in California and the South American Indies you might produce an

ANACONDOR

but decided that you probably wouldn't.

One animal he was glad
to meet for the first time
was the AUK

which sounds a little like
HAWK

and also a little like
YAK

but doesn't look much
like either of them.

Wally made up a rhyme
about the Auk:

The Auk
Is auk-
ward
When he walks,
And when he
Talks,
He talks
In squawks:

Awk!   Awk!

In the course of his word hunt Wally met
a number of imaginary creatures.
CENTAUR (which is only half an
animal) and CHIMERA (which is really
three animals).
Also the ROC, the UNICORN, the
PHOENIX, and the CHESHIRE CAT.
"It's a funny thing," thought Wally,
"these animals aren't alive. They live only
in the Dictionary and the imagination.
Yet they'll still be alive in those two
places thousands of years from now, when
lots of real animals may have died out entirely...."

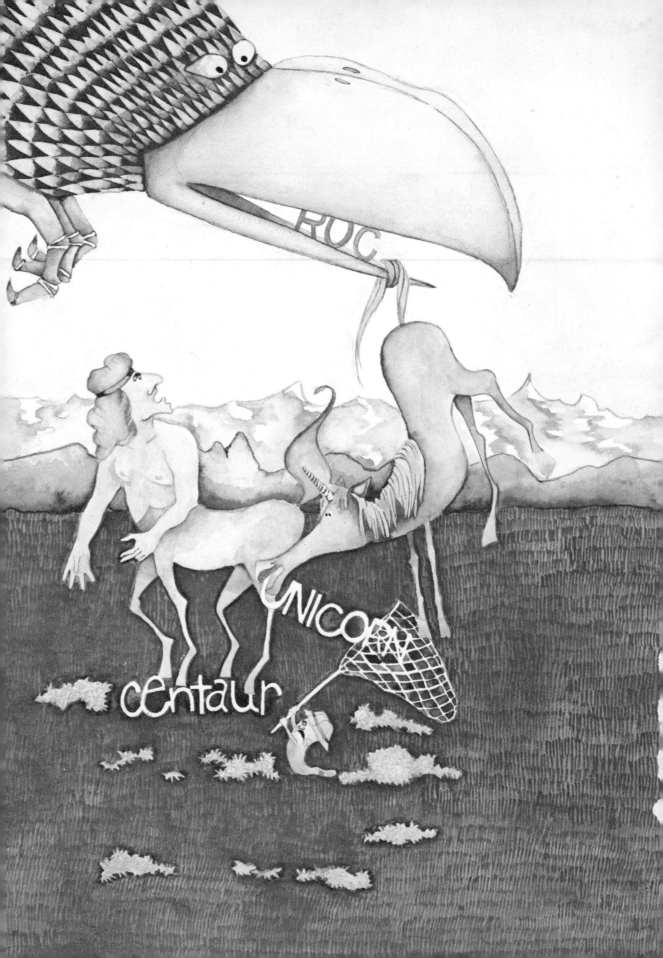

"Hmmm." Wally shook his brain. Such deep thinking tired him. He decided he needed a little food to pick up his spirits. Quickly and deftly, he swallowed a very small word indeed, and also a small lizard.

A few pages later he came to

The "up" and "down" of it sounded ticklish so he ate ESCALATOR, too, and the EFT got a free ride—both bound for the inside, or

interior,

of Wally.

When Wally came to L he was careful to avoid LARK (the one with feathers). He knew all about early birds and worms.

"MOA is no MOA"

One bird he did enjoy was the MOA.

It sounded almost as odd as AUK.
Even odder was the fact that MOA,
according to the Dictionary, was *extinct*.
That means there are no more Moas.
"The Moa is no moa," said Wally to
himself, happily.

PTARMIGAN

which is a kind of grouse, which is a kind
of bird, was Wally's next discovery. He
had never before met a word beginning
with *pt*. He tried to pronounce it
without spitting.

"Pttt pterrible!" said Wally and finally
read the fine print. The Dictionary said
to pronounce it without the *p*, just *tarmigan*.
He threw away the *p* and tarmigan
went down nicely.

Wally's word hunt among the animals
was almost over now. He had bored and
slid and wound his way around to the
very last letter of the alphabet, where he
met his old friend,

ZEBRA

"Not bad," said Wally, taking a lick.
"Sort of a stripy taste, like a
peppermint candy cane."

ZERO

was Wally's last treat for the day. "Tastes like nothing at all," he said, and with a gulp sat down on the last page to think about all he had discovered— hundreds of words, some peculiar, some funny, all interesting.

He'd made great friends with words that were *honest,* words that sounded just like their meanings.

gulp

or

MELLIFLUOUS

which sounds as smooth as honey, and guess what it means.

BABBLE

a babbley
kind of word.

babble
babble
babble
babble
babble
babble
babble
babble
babble
babble
babble
babble
babble
babble
babble
babble
babble
babble
babble
babble
babble
babble

HICCUP

(At first Wally thought HICCUP
was some kind of cup, just as he
had thought CARBUNCLE
was some kind of uncle.)

Then there were lots of words just the other way round—they sounded like one thing but turned out to be another. For example, ZANZIBAR!

Wally thought, "What a good name for a candy bar," and was quite surprised when he found out what it meant.

He was even more surprised when he met
GINGERLY, which he thought (who
wouldn't?) had something to do with
ginger, of which he was very fond. But
GINGERLY didn't.

5280 ft.
1760 yds.

Wally was also fond
of riddles.
He remembered
those old ones:
"What's the longest word
in the English
language?"
Answer: "SMILES"
because there's a mile
between the first letter
and the last."

And,

"What word, if you
reverse the position of
two letters, changes into
its opposite?"
Answer:
"UNITED and
UNTIED, of course."

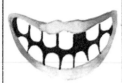

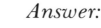

U _ _ _ _ _ D
U _ _ _ _ _ D

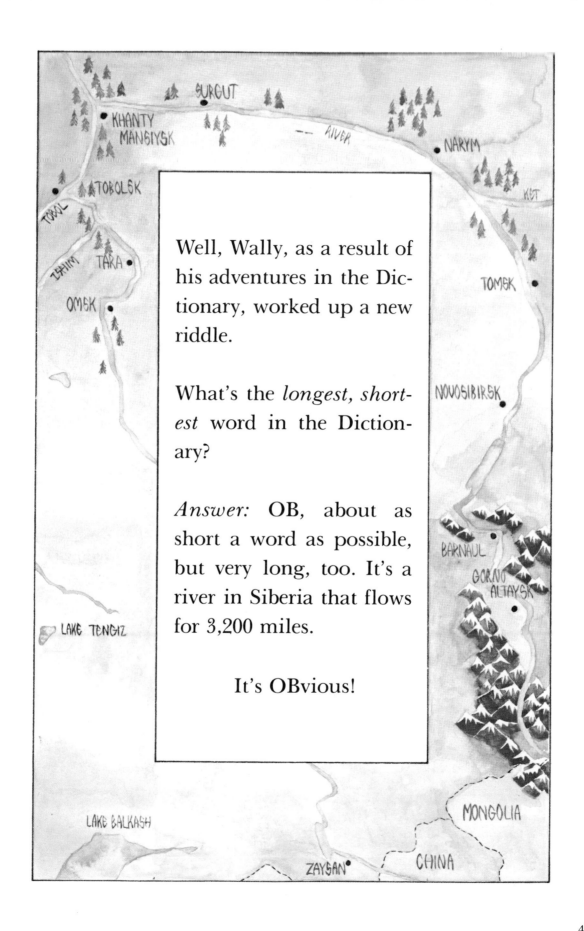

Well, Wally, as a result of his adventures in the Dictionary, worked up a new riddle.

What's the *longest, shortest* word in the Dictionary?

Answer: OB, about as short a word as possible, but very long, too. It's a river in Siberia that flows for 3,200 miles.

It's OBvious!

After so many hours of turning pages, and boring his way through hard words, all Wally could say was

fatiguing

FADING
LONG
TIRED

He wasn't tired of *words*. Far from it.
He was sure he would *never*
get tired of words, the noises they
made, the pictures they painted…
And that was the problem.
It had been a long day
and the light was fading.

He
waved
good-bye
to
ZYMURGY
and
crawled
away
singing.

WALLY'S WORDSONG

by
W. Wordworm

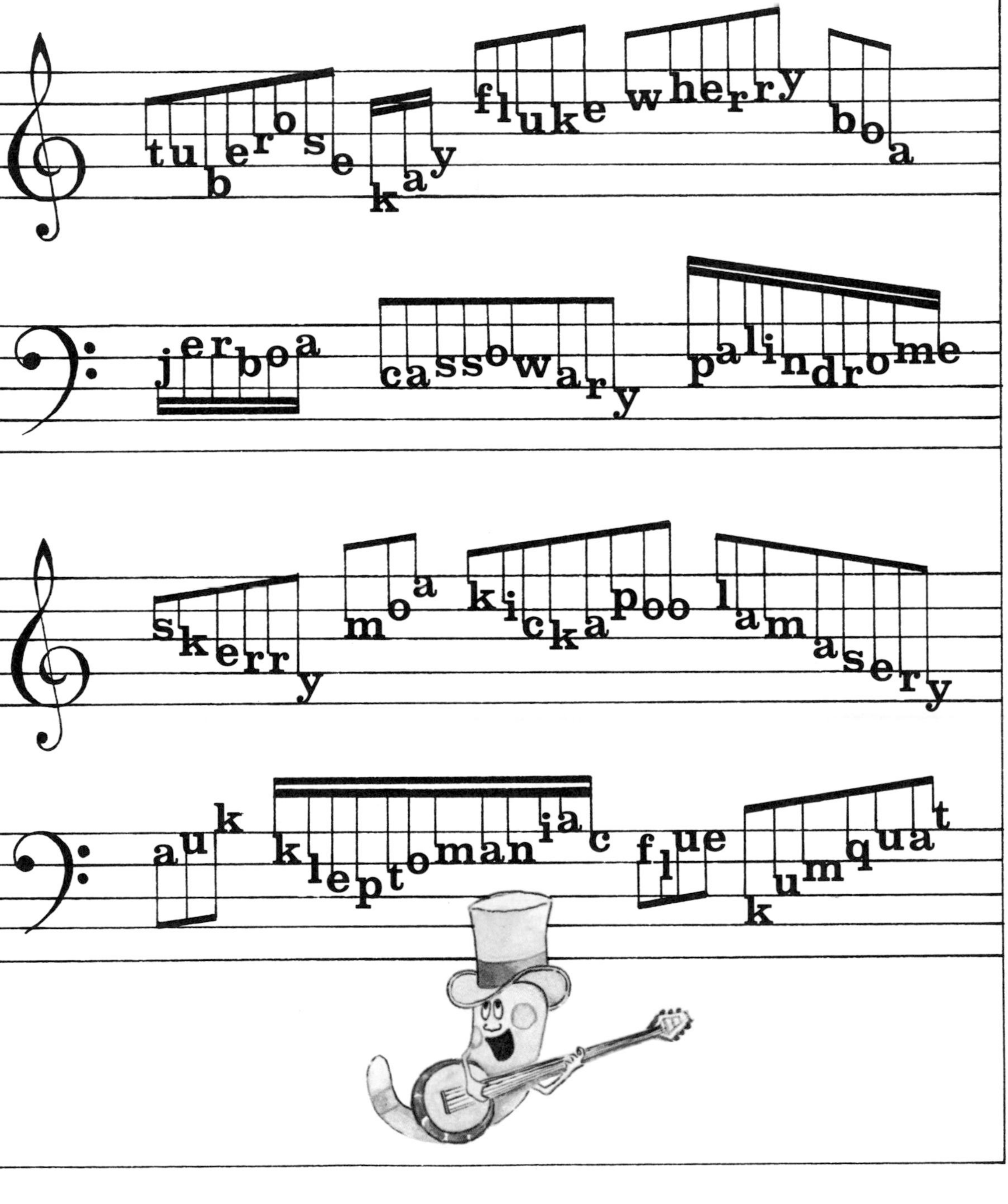

The Auk and the Yak and the Cassowary—
They're all to be discovered in the Dic-tion-ary!
So's the Jerboa. So's the Moa.
And so are the Boa and the Protozoa,
And words my father and mother say,
Like "Income Tax" and "P.T.A."

So—*down* with the books
                that treat me like a baby!
Chuck 'em out the window
                and I don't mean maybe!
I'll tell you the conclusion
                I have come to. It is that
I am *tired* of the cat
                who is sitting on the mat.

A'ses and Z'ses

Kay

I know my A'ses and I know my Z'ses,
And I can pronounce all kinds
 of diseases.
Who was Kay? And *where* is Kew?
And *what* is Kale? You *don't?* I do.

Kew   Kale

I'm the only worm on the block
who knows
What Palindromes are—and
Punctilios,
Or who knows that a Tuberose
isn't a Rose.
I'm the only worm on the block
who *knows!*

Punctilio

Wally

Tuberose

53

Wherry

Lamasery

Skerry

Flue

A Skerry and a Wherry
and a Lamasery
Are all to be found
in the Dic-tion-ary,
Along with a Flume
and a Fluke and a Flue,

Flume

Fluke

Kleptomaniac | Kickapoo

Kumquat Wally

Klep-to-ma-ni-ac!
       Kick-a-poo!
Klieg lights!
       Kumquat! Kokomo!
I'll never have to wonder
       what they are.
           I *know!*

Klieg Lights | Kokomo

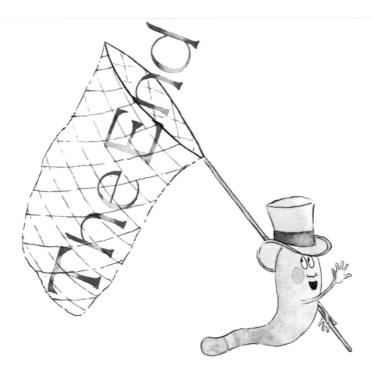

Designed by Barbara Holdridge
Composed in Baskerville Phototype by
    Service Composition, Baltimore, Maryland
Color separations by Capper, Inc., Knoxville, Tennessee
Printed on Northwest Bookbinders Matte by
    Rae Publishing Co., Inc., Cedar Grove, New Jersey
Bound in Devon Green and Multicolor Antique Thistle,
with Multicolor Antique Muscatel endpapers, by
    Rae Publishing Co., Inc., Cedar Grove, New Jersey

DATE DUE

24 COLLIER HEIGHTS

J   CHB
Fadiman, Clifton
Wally the Wordworm